The Adventures of

Ermintrude

The Adventures of
Ermintrude

Eric Thompson

The stories of *The Magic Roundabout*

Originally created by Serge Danot
in a series entitled *Le Manège Enchanté*

BLOOMSBURY

IN THE SAME SERIES

THE ADVENTURES OF DOUGAL
THE ADVENTURES OF BRIAN
THE ADVENTURES OF DYLAN

First published in 1998

Copyright © Eric Thompson 1968–1975
Copyright © Serge Danot/AB Productions SA
Licensed by Link Licensing

Bloomsbury Publishing Plc, 38 Soho Square, London, W1V 5DF

A CIP catalogue record for this book is available from the British Library

10 9 8 7 6 5 4 3 2 1

ISBN 0 7475 4247 3

Typeset by Dorchester Typesetting Group Ltd
Printed in Great Britain by Clays Ltd, St Ives plc

These stories are transcripts of the *Magic Roundabout* TV series that appeared on television in the late sixties and early seventies, as narrated and written by Eric Thompson.

Monster Day

Today is monster day,' said Zebedee, 'but remember there are monsters and monsters.'

And he laughed and he was gone.

Florence and Dougal weren't quite sure what he meant, but then they saw it.

'It's not a monster,' said Florence, 'it's a cow . . . Hello, cow.'

'Hello,' said the cow, and she mooed, contentedly.

'Come and say hello, Dougal,' said Florence.

'I'm not saying hello to a flower-eating monster,' said Dougal.

And he darts quickly behind a tree.

I don't eat flowers, he thought, so why should monsters?

Florence comes to look for Dougal, who runs up a tree.

But it is possible that he was still just a little bit frightened.

'Come down, Dougal,' said Florence. 'Cow says she'll take us to see the pretty flowers – special ones that she doesn't eat.'

But Zebedee said it was time to go home.

Ermintrude's Friend

Mr Rusty was complaining that he had to be a station master again.

'You can do it,' said Zebedee.

'Of course he can,' said Florence.

Florence was waiting for the others on the train platform.

'Where are we going?' asked Dougal.

'We are going to see a friend of yours,' said Florence, with a little (secret) smile.

Mr Rusty was worrying again. 'I can't remember what to do,' he said.

'You wave your flag,' said the train.

'Oh yes,' said Mr Rusty, 'I wave the flag, the flag.'

So he did.

And the train obediently leaves the station.

'Moo,' said Ermintrude, eyeing the train.

'Good morning, Ermintrude,' said Florence, 'we've come to see you.'

'Good morning, Florence,' said Ermintrude. 'Is Dougal with you? I'm longing to see him again.'

'I'm sure he feels the same,' said Florence, looking around, 'but I'm not sure where he is.'

'There he is!' said Ermintrude, seeing Dougal peering

out of a van.

'No I'm not,' said Dougal, shutting the van door.

'Come out, Dougal,' said Florence, 'she won't hurt you.'

'She won't get the chance,' said Dougal in a muffled voice.

'Come on, Dougal,' said Florence.

But as Dougal wouldn't come out Florence thought of a *plan*.

As the train moves on, Florence and the cow pretend to leave, and hide.

'Where have they all gone?' said Dougal, looking out

of the van.

Curious, he gets out, warily. Only to find that they hadn't actually left.

And the plan worked. And they laughed and it made Dougal more nervous than ever.
'They're treating me like a dog,' said Dougal.
And it was time to go home.

An Ayrshire Dragon

Florence arrived at the Roundabout and met Mr Rusty.

'What's that you've got?' Mr Rusty asked.

'It's a book,' said Florence.

Zebedee arrived. 'Doing a little reading?' he said.

'Yes,' said Florence.

'You're not the only one,' said Zebedee, significantly. 'There's some reading going on in the garden too.'

'Really?' said Florence 'That's unusual.'

'I'll say,' said Zebedee.

Dougal was the one who had been reading . . . all about Don Quixote and his horse Rosinante.

'Let's see, er . . . he was followed by his faithful servant Sancho Panza. Now I need a faithful servant,' said Dougal.

Fortunately, just then Brian enters . . .

'Hello,' said Brian. 'Did you know you've got a plate on your head?'

'Never mind about that,' said Dougal. 'I've got a little job for someone. I need a faithful servant.'

'Have you tried the labour exchange?' said Brian.

'I don't need *them* – I've got *you*,' said Dougal.

'Me?' said Brian.

'You. Come here. Look at this,' said Dougal. And he told Brian all about Don Quixote and Sancho Panza.

'It doesn't sound very *me*,' said Brian.

'Silence,' said Dougal, 'and join me in my quest.'

'Oh, I quite like a quest,' said Brian.

Ermintrude saw the quest arriving and got a little agitated.

'Are we questing for anything in particular?' said Brian.

'Silence on the quest,' said Dougal, 'and give me the book.'

'Ah!' said Dougal. 'First – the dragon!'

Ermintrude denied being a dragon.

'Charge!' shouted Dougal.

'I'm an Ayrshire!' said Ermintrude.

'Yes,' said Dougal, 'an Ayrshire dragon! The worst sort – why've we stopped?'

'I'm tired,' said Brian.

'Why pick on me, dears?' said Ermintrude.

'I don't know,' whispered Brian.

'No whispering on the quest,' said Dougal.

'What's he doing, dear?' whispered Ermintrude.

'He's being Don Quixote,' said Brian.

'Might I trouble my faithful servant to get back here – on the double!' said Dougal.

'Surely Don Quixote . . .' said Ermintrude.

'Yes, what about him?' asked Dougal.

'Didn't he have a lady love?' said Ermintrude.

'Oh dear,' said Dougal. 'Come on, we'd better get out of here – fast.'

'Yes, Don,' said Brian.

'Stop!' said Dougal. 'Stop! What's that I see?'

'I dunno,' said Brian. 'What – do you mean that windmill?'

'Giants!' said Dougal. 'Charge!'

Florence arrived . . .

'Ermintrude!' said Florence.

'Esmerelda, dear. The lady love of Don Quixote. Dear man,' said Ermintrude.

'Oh,' said Florence.

Meanwhile . . .

Florence saw a very strange sight. Dougal had charged the windmill and had come off decidedly second best.

'What's happened?' said Florence.

'It's a long story . . .' said Brian.

'Oooooh. Oooooh,' said Dougal.

'What have you been up to, Dougal?' said Florence.

'I'd rather not go into it if you don't mind,' said Dougal, heavily.

'Well, I've brought you a book to read,' said Florence.

'What is it? *War and Peace*?' asked Dougal.

'Yoo! Hoo!' said Ermintrude. 'Look what I've got!'

'She's gone dotty . . .' said Dougal. 'But she's got sugar.'

And not being a dog to turn down an offer of sugar, he graciously accepts it.

'Thank you,' said Dougal, 'I wonder if Don Quixote had an Ayrshire for a girlfriend.'

'Yoo! Hoo!' said Ermintrude.

'I'm terribly confused,' said Brian.

Going Sailing

Dougal had built himself a yacht.

'Going boating?' said Brian.

'It's a land yacht,' said Dougal, 'the latest thing.'

'Oh,' said Brian.

'But I do need wind,' said Dougal.

'Can't you huff at it?' said Brian.

'I'll huff at you if you're not careful, you soppy clump,' said Dougal.

'Only trying to be helpful, old yachter,' said Brian.

'Huh! That'll be the day,' said Dougal.

'Why don't you telephone Mr Heath – he's good at yachts,' said Brian.

'I imagine he's got other things on his mind,' said Dougal, testily.

Meanwhile Florence was meeting Zebedee.

'What a lovely day,' she said.

'Too lovely for some people, I imagine,' said Zebedee.

'Whatever do you mean?' said Florence.

'Go and see,' said Zebedee.

Dougal was feeling very frustrated. '*Typhoons* when you don't want them,' he grumbled.

'How true,' said Brian.

But just then . . .

'A wind! A wind! Oh,' said Dougal.

'Sorry dears . . . Ah . . . Ah . . . Ah . . . Tissoo . . .!' said Ermintrude.

'Could I trouble you for another sneeze?' said Dougal.

'I'm sorry,' said Ermintrude, 'but I think my cold's better now.'

'That was quick,' said Brian.

'I'm a tough old thing, dear,' said Ermintrude.

'Please try,' said Dougal.

'What?' said Ermintrude.

'Sneezing . . . ooo . . .' said Dougal.

'Hey,' said Brian.

Brian whispers in Dougal's ear.

'Really?' said Dougal. 'Ooo!'

Brian and Dougal laugh and Brian leaves.

'Follow!' said Dougal.

'Follow . . . follow . . . follow,' sang Ermintrude.

Florence arrived.

Dougal and Florence go yachting while Ermintrude provides the necessary wind assistance.

'I'm exhausted . . .' said Ermintrude.

But luckily a real wind blew up . . .

'Help!' cried Dougal, picking up speed alarmingly.

Dougal is blown to the cliff edge, where he stops, fortunately.

'That could have been very nasty,' said Dougal.

Dougal takes off.

'Aahhh!' said Dougal.
'Time for bed?' said Florence.

The Clean-Up

Dougal had decided that the garden could do with a little cleaning up.

'It's like a very untidy rubbish dump around here,' said Dougal, 'and you don't help much either.'

'I don't know what you mean,' said Brian.

'Come here,' said Dougal.

'I'm coming, I'm coming,' said Brian.

'I'm going to clean this place up . . . and you're going to help me,' said Dougal.

Dougal showed Brian his vacuum cleaner . . .

'It's the latest model,' he said, 'battery driven, fully transistorised, automatic and extremely expensive. So don't mess about with it . . . all right? Right . . . here we go . . . just try it out, now let's see . . .' said Dougal.

He looks closer.

'Press to start,' said Dougal, 'Ooh . . . very good.'

'Aah!!' said Brian, disappearing suddenly.

'Where's he gone? Now that is *typical* . . .' said Dougal.

The vacuum cleaner goes out of control . . .

'Come back, you idiot machine,' said Dougal.

'It's gone mad . . . mad!' said Dougal.

Meanwhile, Florence was meeting Zebedee.

'I'm going to do some cleaning,' she said.

'You're not the only one,' said Zebedee, laughing a little.

'Why are you laughing?' said Florence.

'You'll see,' said Zebedee.

Dougal flies above Ermintrude. . .

'Oh dear . . . what's that?' said Ermintrude, backing away.

Dougal lands with a screech of brakes.

'Get back, you naughty thing you!' said Ermintrude.

Dougal tried to get back . . . and stopped.

'PHEW!!' said Dougal.

'Now I've heard of spring cleaning but this is ridiculous,' said Ermintrude.

'It's not my fault,' said Dougal.

'You were driving, dear,' said Ermintrude.

'I wasn't driving, it's a vacuum cleaner,' said Dougal.

'What?' said Ermintrude.

'A vacuum cleaner. I'm trying to clean this place up . . . it's like a cow stall,' said Dougal.

'Choose your words, dear boy,' said Ermintrude.

'Oh, sorry,' said Dougal.

He switched the cleaner on again.

And chaos ensues, again . . .

'MOO,' said Ermintrude.

'Oh dear,' said Dougal.

'That thing's *lethal*, dear,' said Ermintrude.

'Hang on,' said Dougal, and he pressed the reverse button.

With a whoosh and a clatter, the cleaner expels Brian, among other things.

'I feel I have been put upon,' said Brian.
'Where've you been?' said Dougal. 'Never here when you're wanted.'
Florence arrived with her feather dusters . . .
'It's cleaning time,' she said.
'Oh what jolly fun and joy and bliss,' said Brian.
'Is this edible?' asked Ermintrude examining the dusters.
'I don't feel like cleaning any more,' said Dougal.

'Just get on with it,' said Florence.

'I know I shall get housemaid's knee . . . anyone want a daily dog?' said Dougal.

Roundabout Trouble

Mr Rusty told Florence a terrible thing . . . the Roundabout had gone wrong and there was nothing he could do to put it right.

'It's a terrible thing,' he said, 'I mean, I'm the custodian. It means *everything* will go wrong . . . because, look, it's going backwards. Look.'

Florence called to Zebedee . . . (BOING) and Ermintrude appeared.

'Gracious,' said Florence.

'You see?' said Mr Rusty.

'What shall we do?' said Florence.

'Suffer, I'm afraid,' said Mr Rusty.

'Brace up,' said Florence.

'I can't,' said Mr Rusty.

'Well, something's got to be done,' said Florence, 'so I'd better do it.'

'You're very brave,' said Mr Rusty.

'What about me, dear?' said Ermintrude.

'Well, you'd better come with me,' said Florence.

In the garden everything was upside down.

Oh dear, thought Florence.

Dougal was there . . .

'Sugar, Dougal?' said Florence.

'Sugar?' said Dougal. 'Never touch it! Absolute poison!'

Poison!

'What's going on, Dougal?' said Florence.

'Everything's quite normal,' said Dougal.

'Oh dear,' said Florence.

'Goodbye!' said Brian.

'Goodbye?' said Florence.

'Well you've just arrived, haven't you?' said Brian.

Brian laughs, speeds off and crashes into the house.

'Oh dear,' said Florence, again.

Things did seem a little chaotic. And Florence wondered what else could possibly go wrong. She soon found out. Mr MacHenry was picking flowers instead of planting them, and behaving very oddly.

'Oh dear,' said Florence, once more.

'Yoo! Hoo! . . . Yoo! Hoo!' said Ermintrude.

Ermintrude flies above Florence.

'Hello dear!' said Ermintrude.

'Oh dear,' said Florence.

Dylan was behaving strangely too: he was chopping down the very tree he usually used to sleep against.

Dylan chops and falls to the ground.

Florence was at her wits' end. She called to Zebedee. Who came.

'What's the matter?' said Florence.

'Wish I knew,' said Zebedee.

Must do something, thought Florence.

And she grabbed Zebedee. And told him about Dylan.

And Mr MacHenry . . . and how everything seemed to be topsy-turvy.

'I know,' said Zebedee.

'Do something,' said Florence.

'I'll try,' said Zebedee.

Dylan got back to normal.

He stops chopping and decides to have a quick nap under the tree.

'That's better,' said Florence.

Zebedee left.

'What's been going on?' said Brian.

'Trouble with the Roundabout,' said Florence. 'I hope everything is all right now . . .'

'What's been going on?' said Dougal. 'Everyone gone dotty?'

'You too, Dougal,' said Florence.

'Me too? What do you mean me too . . . I'm quite normal,' said Dougal.

'Sugar, Dougal?' said Florence.

Dougal slurps gratefully.

'Thank you,' said Dougal.

'Well, *I'm* normal,' said Dougal, 'but I don't think we can say that about *everyone*.'

'Yoo! Hoo! Yoo! Hoo!' said Ermintrude.

'Everything all right?' said Zebedee.

'More or less . . .' said Florence.

'What do you mean "more or less"? I put everything right, didn't I? Like I usually do? Clever old me,' said Zebedee.

Five Miles an Hour

The train had decided there was too much speeding about in the garden. So she imposed a speed limit.

Signs read '5 miles an hour'.

'That should do it,' she said, reversing at speed.
Ermintrude came along . . .
'Five miles an hour? Very good idea – far too much speed about these days,' said Ermintrude.
The train hid behind a tree to make sure Ermintrude didn't go too fast.
Brian arrived.
'What's this? Five miles an hour? I can't do five miles per hour. I can only do about three – top whack. Oh well, better have a go, I suppose,' said Brian.

Brian makes a big effort to comply.

Dougal arrived.
'Oh dear, what's that pathetic little "aporth" up to now?' said Dougal.

Brian is panting and stops, dispirited.

'Oh . . . still five . . . why can't they make it three . . . it's unfair to snails. I shall write to my MP,' said Brian.

What's he doing? thought Dougal. 'What *are* you up to?' he asked. 'Great oaf!'

'Trying to do five miles per hour,' said Brian.

'Oh really!' said Dougal. 'Get on . . .'

'You're too good to me,' said Brian.

'I know. Are you on?' said Dougal.

'Yes,' said Brian.

'Right,' said Dougal.

And Dougal helped Brian to do five miles an hour.

Florence called to Zebedee. 'I feel very energetic,' she said.

'Just as well,' said Zebedee.

'Really?' said Florence.

Florence arrived in the garden . . .

And found Dougal rushing around agitatedly.

'Lost something?' asked Florence.

'Yes . . . a snail,' said Dougal.

'You mean . . . Brian?' said Florence.

'Do you know any others? I was giving him a ride and he just flew off . . . And now I've lost him . . . my little friend . . .' said Dougal, crying. 'Where can he be?'

'When did he fly off?' asked Florence.

'When we reached eighty,' said Dougal.

'EIGHTY?!' said Florence.

Something appeared on the horizon . . .

Ermintrude and Brian appear in the distance.

'It's him!' said Dougal. 'He's back! Stop!'

Ermintrude stopped . . . without informing Brian.

Brian lands with a thump.

'Are you two all right?' asked Florence.

'Perfectly, dear,' said Ermintrude.

'I'm not,' said Brian.

'Well who cares about you? Oaf!' said Dougal.

'Well I like that,' said Brian. 'Here am I, doing my best to keep up with the speed limit and nothing but abuse do I get. It's rotten.'

'Oh dear,' said Florence, sighing.

The train arrives . . .

'I hope you're not going too slow,' said Dougal. 'You have to keep up around here you know.'

'Those signs are a speed *limit*,' said the train.

'Well why didn't you say so? We're not mind-readers, you know,' said Dougal.

'I feel quite frail,' said Ermintrude. 'And you know whose fault it is.'

'Referrin' to me?' said the train.

'The least you can do is take me home,' said Ermintrude.

Brian climbs aboard.

'I daren't look,' said Brian. 'Oh!'

'Why doesn't he get a bicycle?' said Dougal.

'Don't forget . . . Clunk! Click!' said Ermintrude.

A Sugar Mine

Dougal got his weekly grocer's bill in his letterbox.

'Sugar . . . £63.50?!' mumbled Dougal. 'I don't believe it! I don't believe it! I thought there was a shortage. What am I going to do? I can't afford that. I shall have to go to work. I'll have to win the pools.'

He thinks hard.

'I must do something. Steps will have to be taken . . . yes,' said Dougal.
So Dougal decided to dig for his own sugar.

Luckily, he had just the machine for it outside, and after a rather frantic manipulation of the levers, the earth-mover and Dougal disappear into a hole of their own making . . .

'Wish me luck!' said Dougal.

Florence met Zebedee.
'Hello,' he said.
'Hello,' said Florence.
'Would you believe it possible to spend £63.50 on sugar?' said Zebedee.
'In a year?' said Florence.
'A week!' said Zebedee.

Brian was listening . . .

'What is it, dear?' asked Ermintrude. 'Rabbits?'

'Only if rabbits sing "don't go down the mine, Daddy",' said Brian, laughing.

Florence arrived and wondered where everyone had gone to.

'Do you think it might be an earthquake, dear?' said Ermintrude.

'Hello,' said Florence.

Ermintrude flies gracefully up into the air with a moo . . . and lands with a crash!

Florence asked them what they were doing.

'We're listening,' said Ermintrude.

'What . . . ?' said Florence.

'Listening,' said Brian.

'There's something going on underground,' said Ermintrude.

At which point a tree moves and Ermintrude disappears . . .

'Ahh . . . Oh!' said Ermintrude.

'Where's she gone?' said Florence.

'I daren't think,' said Brian.

Ermintrude's cries echo plaintively.

'Who threw that animal at me?' asked Dougal.

'Not I,' said Florence.

'Well someone did and it's not funny,' said Dougal.

'She landed on me . . . I'll trouble you to get out of my sugar mine, madam,' said Dougal.

'I'd love to dear . . . goodbye,' said Ermintrude.

And she leaps, whistling, out of the hole and lands with an earthshaking crash.

Dougal, alone in his hole again, gleefully continues working . . .

'What's he doing?' asked Florence.

'Looking for sugar,' said Brian.

Dougal found some . . .

'Could you ring the government, please?' said Dougal.

'Why?' said Florence.

'I've found a sugar mine,' said Dougal.

'Under your home,' said Florence.

'Oh dear. I hope I haven't undermined the old homestead,' said Dougal.

'Dougal, you're incorrigible,' said Florence.

'I'm *what*?' said Dougal.

'Hopeless,' said Florence.

'Well at least I won't have to pay £63.50 for sugar . . . well not till the price goes up again anyway,' said Dougal.

Sugar Rescue

'Ah, that's better!' said Dougal, slurping thirstily. 'Hey, it's very hot. Unusual for the time of year . . .'

'Hey – your sugar's melting,' said Brian.

'What?! Oops, I shall have to do something about this,' said Dougal.

'Sell it,' said Brian.

'*Sell* it?! Go into *trade*? You must be dotty,' said Dougal.

'Well, you'd better do something or it'll be a soggy mass,' said Brian.

Dougal saw the sense of this. 'I'll put it in the fridge,' he said.

Luckily there happened to be a very big deep freeze to hand. Fully automatic.

Dougal puts the sugar into the fridge . . . and the fridge starts to rumble and shake rather alarmingly . . .

'What?! What . . . ? What?' said Dougal.

Brian retreats hastily outside and hides behind a tree.

'I don't think it likes it,' said Brian.

'Then it can lump it,' said Dougal, joining him.

'Oh, very droll,' said Brian. 'I just hope it doesn't blow up.'

'Why should it blow up? It's a deep freeze, isn't it? It's supposed to freeze anything,' said Dougal.

'Perhaps it hasn't got a sweet tooth,' said Brian.

'Oh . . . don't talk rubbish,' said Dougal.

'Well I hope we don't regret it, that's all,' said Brian.

'Tea for two,' sang Ermintrude.

'Shostakovich, I presume?' said Dougal, laughing.

'Scoff not, dear, or I'll sing it again,' said Ermintrude.

'Spare us,' said Dougal.

'I could give you "I'm forever blowing bubbles",' said Ermintrude.

And she takes to the air with a WHEE! . . . and lands with a splash.

'What did she do that for?' said Dougal.

'Perhaps she was hot,' said Brian.

'Ah!' said Dougal. 'That's the way to keep the sugar cool . . . under water . . . see? Simple.'

'There's got to be a snag there somewhere,' said Brian.

Dougal got his sugar out of the deep freeze.

'Er . . . won't sugar melt under water?' said Brian.

But Dougal wasn't listening.

'Don't put any more of that stuff in 'ere – OK?' said the freezer.

'Charming,' said Dougal.

'Whoops!' said Brian.

Dougal loaded his sugar into his special underwater machine.

'How long have you had this?' said Brian.

Florence was waiting for Zebedee. He arrived.

'Isn't it hot?' said Florence.

'Yes, it is rather,' said Zebedee. 'I should go and cool off if I were you.'

Florence went to the garden to cool off . . . but she couldn't find anyone. Except Ermintrude.

'They're all under the water there, dear,' said Ermintrude.

'Why?' asked Florence.

'Well they're doing some very funny things with sugar . . .' said Ermintrude. 'I'll go and see.'

Ermintrude dives in.

Dougal and Brian (*cruising the water in their propelled machine*) looked for Ermintrude.

'See her?' said Dougal.

'No . . . perhaps she's turned into a mermaid,' said Brian.

'Oh, please talk sense – where would she put her tail? Ooh, what's that?' said Dougal.

'Just checking, dears,' said Ermintrude, and she rose to the surface.

'Yes, they're there,' said Ermintrude to Florence. 'And coming up.'

They arrived.

'What *are* you two doing?' said Florence.

'We're not doing anything . . . we've stopped,' said Dougal.

Wishing Day

Florence said hello to Mr Rusty and Mr Rusty said hello to Florence.

'Oh, I wish I was in the garden,' said Florence.

Whereupon she suddenly disappears.

'Goodness gracious . . . what a strange thing,' said Mr Rusty.

'Any wish you'd like?' said Zebedee.

'No, I'm fine,' said Mr Rusty, hastily.

'Well it's wishing day,' said Zebedee, 'and I've supplied a wishing machine.'

The wishing machine was in the garden and it looked a bit like – a wishing machine.

'Hello, Dougal,' said Florence.

'What's that funny-looking object?' said Dougal.

'No idea,' said Florence.

There is a strange noise from the machine, and Brian appears.

'Hello,' said Brian. 'You know, I was just wishing I was here . . .'

The machine rumbles again, and feathers start to appear on Brian . . .

'What do you think you're doing?' said Dougal.

'I was just *thinking*,' wailed Brian.

'Ooh . . . ooh . . . ooh,' said Brian, as he starts to grow a beard. 'I don't think this is funny.' And he leaves.

'He'll get arrested,' said Dougal.

The garden birds got a bit worried about Brian, as well they might . . .

'Brian?' said Mr MacHenry.

'Yes?' said Brian.

'But you've got a beard and feathers,' said Mr MacHenry. 'Did you know? Er . . . what's going on?'

'I wish I knew,' said Brian, heavily.

Mr MacHenry thought and thought . . . Possibly about the wrong thing.

And with a rumbling noise . . .

Brian returned to normal.

'I'll never understand this programme,' he muttered.

Mr MacHenry wasn't too sure either. And neither was Ermintrude.

There is a crash and Mr MacHenry suddenly appears.

'I wish I had my bicycle,' said Mr MacHenry. And he had.

'Good heavens,' he said.

'Well, moo,' said Ermintrude.

Dylan had wished for carrots and was so overcome he fell asleep.

'Something's going on here,' said Ermintrude.

Florence wished for some flowers . . .

'Why didn't you wish for something useful?' said Dougal.

Brian flies happily past . . .

Brian had obviously had another wish.
'Ooh . . . I am enjoying myself,' he said.
'Oooh!' said Brian, landing awkwardly.
'Now listen,' said Ermintrude, 'I'm right up in the air about this . . .'
And she was.
'I am not amused, dears,' said Ermintrude, flying. 'Now I've no wish to complain but . . .'

The now-familiar rumbling noise is greeted with the arrival of a surprisingly large number of carrots . . .

'Ooo . . . Oh! Oh!' said Ermintrude.
Florence said the wishes were obviously getting mixed up . . .
'Well, *I* wished for sugar,' said Dougal. He got it.
'That's better!' he said.
But wishes can go wrong. Dougal got more sugar than he bargained for . . .
'That'll do . . . that'll do . . . I said . . . that . . . that'll do . . . yes, thank you, that'll do,' said Dougal.

He looks at the mountain of sugar . . .

'I feel sick,' said Dougal.

The Number 12

Ermintrude is drumming with her hooves. As cows do . . .

'Roll up! Roll up! I have a special announcement. To me, everyone! To me! Come along! Don't be shy! Now where *is* everyone? Never here when you want them,' said Ermintrude.

'To me, everyone! To me!' said Ermintrude again.

The drum breaks under Ermintrude's energetic assault.

'Oh dear,' said Ermintrude.

Dylan arrived to see what all the fuss was about and he asked Ermintrude to give him a ride.

'You'll have to pay, dear,' said Ermintrude.

'Pay?' said Dylan. 'Like . . . pay?'

'Of course,' said Ermintrude.

'Oh no, ma'am – why pay?' said Dylan.

'I'm a bus. Now get off,' said Ermintrude.

Dougal decided to take action.

'Now wait a moment,' he said. 'Now wait just one moment. What's all this about being a bus?'

'Oh, are you a bus?' said Brian. 'What's your number?'

'I'm a 12,' said Ermintrude. 'Let's all go down the Strand,' she sang.

Ermintrude leaves with the noise of a bus.

'Poor old thing – thinks she's a bus,' said Dougal.

Florence arrived . . .

'Oh! Er . . . oh hello . . .' said Ermintrude, as she passed her noisily.

The train arrived. 'Hellooo!' said the train.

'Oh . . . Oh hello, dear thing,' said Ermintrude.

'And what might you be doing . . . if I may make so bold, madam,' said the train.

'I'm a bus. A number 12,' said Ermintrude. 'Let's all go down the Strand . . .'

'May I have a word?' said the train.

'Of course,' said Ermintrude. 'Any amount, dear thing.'

The train got rather agitated . . . 'I want no buses on my patch,' she said, acidly.

'Oh, come now,' said Ermintrude.

But the train wouldn't listen – and she went off in a huff. 'Buses indeed!' she said. 'Whatever next?'

'Oh dear,' said Ermintrude. 'No wonder she was nationalised. Ah well . . . I'll just have to show her.'

Ermintrude passes the train, and then stops.

'I've got time for a snack – and I'll still beat her to Southend,' said Ermintrude.

The train toots and startles Mr MacHenry.

'I think I've given her far enough start,' said Ermintrude. There was a confrontation at the crossing.

'I have right of way!' said the train.

'Oh hoity-toity!' said Ermintrude.

'Now, ladies, this will not do! Do it will not!' said Dougal.

'Well make her get out of the way of my bus,' said Ermintrude.

'Oh dear,' said Dougal. 'No wonder the country's going to the dogs . . . what am I saying?'

UFOs

'What are you doing, old thing?' said Brian.

'Ha! Ha!' said Dougal. 'You may well ask.'

'What is that? Is it an egg?' asked Brian.

'The way your mind harps on food,' said Dougal.

The train arrived. 'What's that?' she asked.

'I've added something to make it easier,' said Dougal.

'Well if that makes it easier,' said the train, 'I'll get back to Crewe.'

Dylan arrived. 'Like . . . what's . . . what's . . . like *that*?' he asked.

'Oh you're all so *ignorant*,' said Dougal. 'It's a UFO.'

'Uncle's Funny Onion?' said Brian, laughing.

'Unidentified *Fly*ing Object,' said Dougal.

'Oh . . . like . . . flying saucers, man?' asked Dylan, sitting down . . . and going to sleep.

'Exactly,' said Dougal.

'What?' said Brian.

'Flying saucers,' said Dylan. 'Visitors from another planet.'

'From Mars or Venus or Neptune,' said Dougal.

'Or Barnsley?' said Brian.

'Oh this is hopeless,' said Dougal. 'Like explaining to a brick wall.'

'Still looks like an egg to me,' said Brian.

Dougal was on the lookout for visitors from outer space.

Dylan was having a look too – none too hopefully.

Dylan yawns and goes to sleep.

'How do they keep saucers in the air?' mused Dougal.
'Come in, Number Three, your time is up,' said Brian.
Meanwhile, at the Roundabout, Zebedee met Florence.
'Shall we go then?' said Zebedee.
'Why not?' said Florence.
'See some flying saucers,' said Zebedee.
'Flying saucers?' said Florence.

'Well, you never know,' said Zebedee.
'No, you never know,' said Florence.
Dougal was still looking. 'Where've they all got to?'
he said.

'Hello, Dougal,' said Florence. 'Hello, Dougal. Sugar.'

Dougal slurps.

'You're too good to me,' said Dougal.
'I know,' said Florence.
'You haven't seen any, I suppose?' said Dougal.
'He means flying teapots and plates . . . and that,' said Brian.
'Well, there's something odd,' said Florence.
'Odd is right,' said Dougal.
'Hello, dears,' said Ermintrude. 'I'm an easily identified flying thing. I'm a flying cow . . . Up, up and away in my beautiful balloon . . .' she sang, floating upwards.

Ermintrude falls to the ground with a crash.

'All right, Ermintrude?' said Florence.
'Yes thank you, dear . . . just feeling a little light on my feet,' said Ermintrude.
'She's about as light on her feet as a hippo with a sprained ankle,' said Dougal, laughing.
'I heard that dear . . . here I co . . . come,' said Ermintrude.

Ermintrude glides up and sings . . .

'Up, up and away . . .'

Home on the Range

'Well now, howdy folks . . . this is your friendly neighbourhood marshal,' said Dougal.

'You hoo!' said Ermintrude.

'Indians! Oh, no . . . Howdy, mam,' said Dougal, laughing.

'Howdy, dear. Would you like to round me up?' said Ermintrude.

'Certainly not – I'm a sheriff, not a cowboy,' said Dougal.

'Oh, go on,' said Ermintrude.

So Dougal rounded Ermintrude up – just a little.

'Oh . . . is that it, dear?' said Ermintrude.

Florence called to Zebedee. Who arrived.

'Hello,' said Florence.

'Well, hello you,' said Zebedee. 'Shall we go?'

'Why not?' said Florence.

Back in the garden, Ermintrude found herself all tied up.

'What happened to you?' asked Dougal.

'Rustlers, dear – took a fancy to me,' said Ermintrude.

The train arrived. 'Toot toot! Toot toot!'

'Oh . . . am I being rescued, dear old marshal, dear?' said Ermintrude.

'What are you doing to that poor creature?' asked the train. 'Untie her at once, you cruel, heartless beast.'

'It wasn't me,' said Dougal. 'I don't go round tying folk up. Really.'

'Well I think it's a crying shame,' said the train. 'Don't worry, dear – I'll rescue you!'

'Too kind,' murmured Ermintrude.

Brian and Dylan arrived.

'Er . . . can we, like, play too?' said Dylan.

'What do you mean "play"?' said Dougal.

'I like your horse,' said Brian, laughing. 'What's he called, wooden-top?'

'Oh, go on, laugh,' said Dougal. 'Never take anything seriously, do you? Great clump!'

Dougal falls over with a cry.

'I'm still here,' said Ermintrude.

'Give me time,' said Dougal, 'I mean, we can't rush into this, you know . . .'

'But I'm getting crampy,' said Ermintrude. 'In an awkward place.'

'I'm worried about Indians,' said Dougal.

And he was right to worry.

The sound of drums fills the air . . .

'Anyone want to be sheriff?' said Dougal nervously. 'Sheriff?'

'How much?' said Brian.

'Don't be rotten,' said Dougal.

'Charming,' said Brian.

'Well hi!' said Dylan.

He was wearing a big star so Dougal thought he

would make a good sheriff.

Dylan lies down and yawns.

'Well talk about High Noon. Here I am, my friends run off and the sheriff's asleep,' said Brian.

The sound of drums continues.

'Oh help! Help!' said Ermintrude.

The train arrives, heroically.

'I've heard of a wagon train but this is ridiculous,' said Brian.
The train rescued Ermintrude.
'What's the matter, Dougal?' said Florence, arriving at last.
'Run for your life,' screeched Dougal, 'the place is littered with Indians. Sioux . . .'
'Sue?' said Florence. 'What's she doing here?'
'Home, home on the range, where the deer and antelope play,' said Brian.
'Hello, Brian – what's going on?' said Florence.
'Oh, just a little Indian trouble,' said Brian.

And the drumming continues . . .

'Train's late,' said Florence.
'I'm not surprised,' said Brian.
He looks at Dylan.
'That's our sheriff – very quick on the snore,' he said.

Magic Sauce

Dougal had found a box . . . and in the box he'd found a bottle . . . and in the bottle he'd found a note. 'Magic Sauce. One drop and any wish will come true. Take care not to exceed stated dose. Excellent with bacon and eggs. No preservatives,' read Dougal.

Dougal wished for some sugar.

And there it was . . . Or was it?

'Now what's going on here?' said Dougal.

'What you got there?' asked Brian, arriving.

'None of your business,' said Dougal, and he put the note away hastily.

'Oh, I wish I had something to ride on. I'm so tired,' said Brian.

'Well I may be able to help you there,' said Dougal.

'Ooh!' said Brian.

'Have a wish,' said Dougal.

'I just wish I had a snaily bicycle . . . oh!' said Brian.

And there it was . . . a snaily bicycle.

'Another satisfied customer. I hope you've got a licence,' said Dougal.

'Wait a minute,' said Brian. 'Some sugar for you. I knew I had some in my pantry.'

Dougal collected the sugar thoughtfully. 'I think I'm on to a good thing here,' he said, laughing.

Ermintrude arrived. 'Hello, dear boy,' she mooed. 'May I come in?'

'Have you a particular wish,' said Dougal, 'something you've always wanted?'

'Yes,' said Ermintrude. 'I want to go to the moon to see what it's really like.'

'Three lumps of sugar and your wish is granted,' said Dougal.

Dougal holds out the magic bottle . . .

'Have a sniff of that,' said Dougal.

'Oh!' said Ermintrude. 'Oh! I feel so light. I've come over all unnecessary.'

Ermintrude takes off . . .

'Don't forget to pay,' said Dougal.

'Here!' said Ermintrude.

Dougal put the sugar away, chortling.

I'll have enough to last me for life, he thought. And he started to pick some flowers for Florence, who was meeting Zebedee.

Zebedee arrived.

'Shall we go then?' said Florence.

'Go where?' said Zebedee, innocently, laughing a bit.

'Oh, come on,' said Florence, 'you know where.'

Dougal had picked a bunch of flowers for Florence. I think I'll have a lump of sugar while I'm waiting, he thought.

But it was easier said than done. The magic sugar just wouldn't stay still.

'Come back you . . . you . . . lump, you . . . Oh . . .

I'm so furious! What's the good of this?' said Dougal.

Florence arrived and Dougal gave her the flowers.

'Oh, thank you, Dougal,' said Florence.

'Don't mention it,' said Dougal.

Dougal slurps on his sugar.

'Ooh . . . I needed that,' said Dougal. 'Thank you.'

'What's the matter?' said Florence.

'Well it's a long story, but if you've got a couple of days free, I'll tell you,' said Dougal.

'Listen,' said Florence.

'What?' said Dougal.

They hear the noise of a rocket and Ermintrude and Brian fly past . . .

'Hello, dear,' said Ermintrude.

'Hello, dearies,' said Brian.

Dougal thought he'd better have another wish, but before he could do so Zebedee arrived in the box.

'I'd better take this away, hadn't I?' said Zebedee.

'Yes,' said Dougal, heavily.

The bottle and box vanish but some sugar is left behind . . .

'Oh, look Dougal . . .' said Florence.

'I'm looking,' said Dougal.

'Brush your teeth,' said Zebedee.

'Of course,' laughed Dougal. 'Got a brush?'

Supermarkets and Stilton Hotels

At the Roundabout, Florence was waiting for Zebedee.

'Hello,' he said.

'Hello,' said Florence. 'Late again.'

'I am not,' said Zebedee, 'am I?'

'Of course you are,' said Florence.

In the garden Dougal was supervising the latest scheme. He was building a motorway.

Brian was using the latest high-tech, and rather noisy, equipment to clear the route of trees and . . . a rabbit.

'I didn't even wake him up!' said Brian.

Dylan sighs.

'No good will come of this, dear, mark my words,' said Ermintrude. 'Mark my words. Motorways indeed! It'll be supermarkets and stilton hotels next and we all know what happens then, don't we?' said Ermintrude.

'No, what?' said Florence.

'Well, dear, up goes the price of turnips so much a poor creature like myself can't afford them. And that's not all – there'll be a crime wave and buggings and huggings and things of that nature . . .' said Ermintrude.

'Oh, come – it can't be as bad as that,' said Florence.

'Ah, dear, you're so young and trusting. I remember

saying when I was a gal that no good would come of it
all . . . and I was right.'

*Brian starts to move the flowers out of the way of the
proposed motorway.*

'Hurry up!' said Dougal. 'That's better.'
'Is that all right then, foreman and road building
chum?' said Brian.

'I think so,' said Dougal. 'We'll have to test the sur-
face. I'll use my high-powered car.'
Florence arrived – walking along the new road.
'Get off – you'll spoil the surface,' said Dougal.
'I thought it was meant to be a road?' said Florence.

'For everyone.'
  'Well yes,' said Dougal. 'Everyone with a car, that is.'
  'And if you haven't got a car,' said Florence, acidly.
  'Stay at home,' said Brian.

Just then, Ermintrude approaches, driving rather fast. . .

  'Oh dear . . .' said Dougal.

Ermintrude, singing happily, begins pushing the trees back to their pre-motorway positions.

  'Stop it, you mad bovine fool you!' said Dougal.
  'Over here, Ermintrude,' said Florence.
  'I shall stand in her path,' said Brian, bravely.
  'We shall not be moved,' said Brian, on the verge.

Ermintrude continues while Dylan lets out a sigh.

  'I wonder if I should let her tyres down?' said Dougal.
  'That's that,' said Ermintrude.
  'So much for progress,' said Dougal.
  'I would have stood in her way,' said Brian.
  'I have nothing against snails,' said Ermintrude.
  'I told you she was dotty . . .' said Dougal.
  'Home then!' said Ermintrude.
  'I'll trouble you to leave my car here,' said Dougal.
Dylan woke up.
  'Anything been happening?' he asked. 'Like . . .'

Dylan leans over and crashes to the floor.

Jumping Competition

'Are you following me, snail, because if you *are*, cease,'
said Dougal.

'But I'm your chum,' said Brian.

'I should be so unlucky,' said Dougal. 'And anyway I
am preparing for the Olympic Games . . . long jump.
The long jump is only difficult if the landing area is a
long way from the take-off area. Now, I have brought
the two closer together making the long jump – what's
that rabbit doing?'

That rabbit was playing the guitar.

'Cheek!' said Dougal.

The music continues.

'Tell him to go away,' said Dougal.

'He's bigger than me!' said Brian.

Dylan played on . . .

And meanwhile, Zebedee was meeting Florence.

'I hear there are games in the garden,' he said. 'Special
games! Olympic-type games.'

'Oh, good,' said Florence.

'What you doing, Dougal?' said Florence.

'Jumping!' said Dougal.

'Jumping!' said Florence.

'Me too,' said Brian.

'No you're not!' said Dougal. 'He's not!'

'I am! I am!' said Brian.

Dylan decided not to jump . . .

'I'm a great jumper,' said Brian.

'Modest little soul, aren't you? Great oaf!' said Dougal.

Mr MacHenry came in, lit the Olympic flame, and left.

'I'm glad everyone's taking so much interest,' shouted Dougal.

So Mr MacHenry came back. 'That's all right,' he said.

'Can't we start?' said Brian.

'You'll need a start,' said Dougal, laughing.

'Oh dear,' he said, spotting the seated Dylan.

Dylan was prepared to play the Olympic fanfare.

'I presume nothing I do or say will stop you,' said Dougal, and he was right.

Dylan trumpets the fanfare, gets up, and leaves.

'Perhaps we can get on now,' said Dougal, and he showed Florence the Olympic medals for the long jump . . . and the winners' rostrum, next to the Olympic House.

'It's all very epic,' said Brian, 'but what about a bit of jumping?'

'Oh, yes,' said Dougal.

His idea for making the long jump easier impressed Florence very much.

Florence applauds as Brian stands ready on a spring-board.

'All suitably agog?' said Brian.

Brian springs noisily off the board and lands with a thud.

'A new British record I think – for snail leaping,' said Brian.
'Very good,' said Florence, applauding.

Dougal decides it's high time he jumped. So he does. Meanwhile . . .

Ermintrude entered silently . . .
'I think I win,' said Dougal.
But Florence wasn't sure and neither was Mr MacHenry.
'I think we should measure,' said Mr MacHenry.

There is a very loud, not to say unexpected, sound of splintering wood.

'Thunder?' said Dougal. 'What? What! What! What!'

Dougal turns and looks at the board. The board is broken and Ermintrude is on the ground.

'Mooooooo,' said Ermintrude, getting up. 'What fun! I am still in cracking form: what's the next event? I'm very good at the hammer throw and my high-jump won the moon event last year. Moo,' said Ermintrude.

The Rainbow

Florence was calling on a part of the garden she'd never seen before, accompanied by Dougal.

'Lovely, isn't it?' she said.

'Bit chocolate-boxy if you ask me,' said Dougal.

'You're so difficult sometimes,' said Florence, getting a bit huffy.

'Oh, getting a bit huffy, aren't we,' said Dougal. 'Miss Huff! OOH!'

They came across some new flowers . . .

'I'm a bit cold,' said Florence.

'Cold?' said Dougal.

'Ooooooo!!' said Florence in fright.

'I'm called Icy Daisy,' said the Flower.

Dougal sniggered.

'Dougal!' hissed Florence.

'Well, Icy Daisy!' said Dougal.

'Icy by name and icy by nature,' said the Flower. 'I can change in a flash so pick me if you dare . . .'

The Flower changes colour . . .

'Oh, we wouldn't do that,' said Florence.

'Why not?' said the Flower.

'Because you told us not to,' said Florence, 'that's why.'

And she sits down.

Dougal laughed.

Florence looked at the trees – dreamily.

'A quarter to six and not a bone boiled,' said Dougal.

He passes the flower.

'Icy Daisy,' said Dougal, laughing.

'Come on, up! Up!' said Dougal.

'Oh, all right, Dougal,' said Florence.

'Call again,' said Icy Daisy.

'You do meet some funny ones,' said Dougal. 'Don't you? Funny ones!'

The two of them walk on, wondering what else they might meet . . .

'And here's another . . . Coo!' said Dougal to the totem pole – for such it was.

'Whatever next?' said Florence.

'It'll talk,' said Dougal.

'Watch it, buster,' said the totem pole.

'Told you,' said Dougal.

The totem pole puffs on a pipe.

'That'll stunt your growth,' said Dougal.

'Pipe of peace!' said Florence.

'Correct, paleface,' said the totem pole.

'Paleface?!' said Dougal, laughing.

Dougal and Florence leave the totem pole.

'I've never been called a paleface,' said Florence.

'Well you have now,' said Dougal. 'Come on, Hinnehaha . . . Why do we keep doing these turns?'

'Paleface,' mused Florence.

'Well you have got a pale face,' said Dougal.

'Yes, I know, but *paleface*,' said Florence.

They met Ermintrude browsing.

'I don't think I can stand it,' said Dougal. 'Been at the flowers again, haven't you?'

'I haven't,' said Ermintrude.

'Oh, you fibber!' said Dougal.

'A couple fell into my mouth, that's all,' said Ermintrude.

'Oh, *Ermintrude*,' said Florence.

'She's past saving,' said Dougal.

'Can I help it if the flowers mix themselves up with the grass?' said Ermintrude.

Dougal had to have some sugar to keep up his strength . . .

Dougal slurps.

'By the way . . .' said Ermintrude.

'Yes?' said Florence.

And then she saw – the rainbow was missing another colour.

'We might have known,' said Dougal. 'It's that cow, that's who it is . . . She can't resist greenery, and put a bit of yellow in and she'll slurp it all . . . true or false? Ter-rue or fer-alse?'

He pauses to get back his breath.

'It's come to a pretty pass when your rainbows get

slurped away by herds of cows . . . really,' said Dougal.

'There's only one,' said Florence.

'Just little me,' said Ermintrude. 'Oh, I love a leaf more than life . . .'

Lost Ball

Florence arrived at the Roundabout and met Mr Rusty.

'I didn't see you,' she said. 'Were you hiding from me?'

'No,' said Mr Rusty.

'Oh,' said Florence.

'I was just oiling the Roundabout – needs oil, you know,' said Mr Rusty.

'Oh, I see,' said Florence.

Zebedee appears, with a boing.

'Going then?' said Zebedee.

'Certainly,' said Florence, happily.

She met Dougal . . .

'I have a question to ask you,' said Dougal.

'Ask away,' said Florence. 'Oh, your nose is cold . . . how funny.'

'What do you mean funny?' said Dougal.

'Mine's warm,' said Florence.

'Probably because you're not a dog,' said Dougal, icily.

'Hadn't thought of that,' said Florence.

'Oh, really!' said Dougal.

Ermintrude was sitting around near by . . .

'Hello,' said Florence.

'Hello, dear things . . .' said Ermintrude. 'Just having

a few flowers for brekky wekky . . . Nothing like a piece of daisy toast and a petunia sandwich,' she added. 'There's just one thing – someone's been trampling about . . .' She notices Dougal.

'Hello, handsome,' Ermintrude said, laughing. 'And it's not good enough. This garden is not for trampling – it's for flower eating and other similar pleasures.'

Ermintrude is interrupted by a very loud noise.

'Whatever's that?' said Ermintrude.
'What indeed?' said Dougal.

A football team marches past . . .

Florence and Ermintrude and Dougal followed.
'I wouldn't fancy their chances against *Fulham*,' said Dougal, laughing.
'There, I knew it,' said Ermintrude. 'Footballers in the garden – whatever next? Is nothing sacred I ask myself. . .'

The team plays and then stops.

'Seen our ball?' said the footballers.
'No,' said Florence.
'No,' said Dougal.
'But we'll all look,' said Florence.
'Huh!' said Ermintrude and Dougal.
'*I'm* not condoning garden trampling,' said Ermintrude.
'Huh . . . *she* can talk!' said Dougal.

Florence looked for the ball. 'Come on, Dougal,' she
said. 'I wonder what it's like.'

'Round,' said Dougal, laughing.

The team practised without a ball.

'Can't find it,' said Florence to the team.

Mr MacHenry arrived.

'What have you got there?' said Florence.

'Something you might find useful,' said Mr MacHenry. 'Have a look . . .'

Mr MacHenry passes Florence a parcel.

And it was something very useful . . .

*She unwraps the parcel to find, surprisingly, a
football.*

'Thank you,' said Florence.

'Happy now?' said Dougal.

And they were . . .

Florence throws the ball to the team.

'Bit late for the World Cup,' said Mr MacHenry.

Zahara's Song

Mr Rusty was talking to himself, like people do sometimes, when Florence arrived.

'Hello,' said Mr Rusty.

'Hello,' said Florence.

Zebedee arrived. 'All well?' he asked.

'Can't complain,' said Mr Rusty.

'Can't complain,' said Florence.

'Good,' said Zebedee. 'It's nice to have satisfied customers.'

Dougal couldn't complain either, although he was working on it.

'Hello, Dougal,' said Florence. 'What's that noise?'

'Ah! I'm glad you asked me that,' said Dougal.

'Then answer,' said Florence.

'My, we're in a pert mood, aren't we?' said Dougal.

But before he could explain the noise, Mr MacHenry came along

'There's a flying creature about,' said Mr MacHenry.

'Oh?' said Florence.

'What sort of flying creature?' said Dougal. 'A winged snail?' *Dougal laughs*.

'Dragonfly,' said Mr MacHenry.

Dougal went quite pale.

'*DRAGON*?' said Dougal.

'Don't see them often,' said Mr MacHenry. 'Pretty

creatures.'

'Oh, yes,' said Florence.

'But there's also a noise, had you noticed?' said Mr MacHenry.

The sound of someone, something, playing the trumpet is heard. And then they see it . . .

'What is it?' said Florence.

'It's outside my experience,' said Mr MacHenry.

'I'm glad it's outside mine,' said Dougal.

'I like it,' said Mr MacHenry.

The dragonfly continues to trumpet energetically.

'Do you think if I gave it sixpence it'd go away?' said Dougal, ungraciously. 'Do you know "The Flight of the Bumble Bee"?' He laughed.

'I think it's nice,' said Florence.

Ermintrude was having a browse . . .

. . . when the dragonfly trumpeted past.

'Hello, dear thing,' she said.

The dragonfly was giving everything and everyone in the garden the benefit of her music.

'Are you free for panto?' said Dougal.

The music continues, to Dougal's annoyance.

'Well it's been a bit more than I can stand,' said Dougal, going under.

'Going under, Dougal?' said Florence.

Zebedee arrived. 'All well?' he said. 'Because I really think it's time for bed.'

So Florence went home to bed, very slowly.

Dougal is left on his own in the garden, when the dragonfly decides to give one final, very loud, rendition.

'I've gone deaf!' said Dougal.

Flamenco

Brian . . . was looking for Dougal. 'Are you there, old matey?' he said.

'Yes,' said Dougal, 'but would you mind not calling me "old matey"?'

'All right, old chum,' said Brian.

'*Nor* "old chum",' said Dougal.

'Well I've got to call you *something*,' said Brian.

'Try "Sir",' said Dougal.

Meanwhile, at the Roundabout, Zebedee looked for Florence and found her.

'There you are,' he said.

'*Comme d'habitude*,' said Florence, in French.

Dougal was waiting . . .

'How's Brian?' said Florence.

'Who on earth cares?' said Dougal.

'I do,' said Florence.

'Well there's no accounting for taste,' said Dougal. 'Now if you'd said "How are *you*, Dougal", I could have seen some sense in it, but to ask after snails . . .'

'Don't go on, Dougal,' said Florence.

'I'm very sorry if I'm boring you,' said Dougal.

Florence sighed . . .

'I mean if I'm boring you just say and I'll go away,' said Dougal.

Just then, they hear singing – energetic, if not musical . . .

'What's that?' said Dougal.
'What a *noise*,' said Florence. 'Whatever can it be?'
'Something's being tortured,' said Dougal.

They walk anxiously in the direction of the noise, and meet Dylan . . . and a bottle which appears to be singing the Flamenco Song.

'Is he quite well?' said Dougal.
'It's the greatest,' said Dylan, 'the *greatest* . . .'
'It's the *loudest*,' said Brian.

Dylan plays guitar while the bottle sings.

'Olé,' said Dougal.

'Oh, it so reminds me of the Costa Brava,' said Ermintrude. 'Olé! Olé! Olé!'

Dougal had an idea . . .

'Olé! Olé! Olé!' said Ermintrude.

'Huh! Toro!' said Dougal, deciding a bull-fight would be interesting – much to Ermintrude's amazement.

'Are you waving that flag at me?' said Ermintrude, preparing to charge.

'Take your time,' said Dougal.

'I'm working myself up into an absolute *frenzy*,' said Ermintrude.

'You could have fooled me,' said Dougal.

'Cheeky thing,' said Ermintrude. 'Don't provoke me or I'll *strike . . . hard.*'

'You haven't *moved* yet,' said Dougal.

'I'll bet Belmonde never has this trouble,' he said, trying again.

Ermintrude waited for the brave bull-fighter to come back . . . paused . . . and charged.

'Get off,' said Dougal.

Ermintrude's Dance

Zebedee arrived at the Roundabout . . . early.

'Early for once, I see,' said Florence, eating an ice-cream.

'You're very cruel to me,' said Zebedee.

'Have a lick,' said Florence.

'No, thank you,' said Zebedee. 'I'm trying to give them up.'

'You are funny,' said Florence.

'I try to please,' said Zebedee. 'Shall we go?'

'Yes,' said Florence.

'All right then,' said Zebedee. 'Be careful of your ice-cream.'

Dougal was busy . . .

'What's that?' said Florence. 'A book?'

'It's a diary I'm keeping,' said Dougal, 'on the habits of rabbits. It's a very important study – I may get a Nobel Prize.'

'Have a lick?' said Florence.

'Most refreshing,' said Dougal.

'What shall we do?' said Florence.

'I can't just stop working,' said Dougal. 'The world awaits my treatise.'

'Can't it wait?' said Florence.

'Well, I suppose I should rest my brain,' said Dougal. 'Come along . . .'

So they went.

'I'd better not leave my diary,' said Dougal. 'There *are* spies about and the world of scholarship is very competitive, and anyway it's got my recipes in it.'

A surprise awaited them . . .

'You know,' said Dougal, 'I've got a funny feeling something's going to happen – a strange foreboding . . .'

Dougal was right . . .

With his next step, he starts to slide across the ground. Eventually, friction takes over, and he shudders to a stop.

'You were right, Dougal,' said Florence, 'something did happen.'

'I *know*,' said Dougal, 'I must make a note . . .'

Dylan came along . . . and skated.

'Interesting,' said Dougal. 'A skating rabbit.'

'Like . . . ice?' said Dylan. 'Crazy . . . crazy.'

'I think there's going to be another happening,' said Florence.

And she was right.

Ermintrude enters, skating to music, and Florence applauds.

'Thank you, darling,' said Ermintrude.

Dougal slips over.

'What am I *doing*?' said Dougal.

'What *are* you doing, Dougal?' said Florence.

Ermintrude continues with her routine.

'I shall have to start a fresh chapter,' said Dougal.
'My next trick is impossible,' said Ermintrude.
'No one would ever believe us,' said Dougal.
Dougal consulted his notes.
'More ice!' said Ermintrude as Brian arrived.
'The ice-man cometh,' said Brian. 'I've done some funny things in my time, but fetching ice in a sack is about the funniest. I have no wish to complain but it is making certain parts of little me rather *numb* – I may never recover. I don't suppose anyone will care – snails are misused little creatures . . . Ah well!'
Dylan started the music again.
'I have another foreboding,' said Dougal.

Ermintrude skates gracefully past . . . and crashes, loudly.

'The ice-man goeth,' said Brian.

Ermintrude's Toothache

Florence called to Zebedee – boing! – who arrived rather gracefully.

'That was rather graceful,' said Florence.

'Do you think so?' said Zebedee.

'Oh, positively *graceful*,' said Florence.

'It's my new spring,' said Zebedee, gracefully. 'Shall we go?'

Florence looked for Dougal, who arrived.

'I'm here,' he said. 'Let joy be unconfined.'

'Who's Joy?' said Florence.

'Don't tell me it's going to be one of those days,' said Dougal.

And Florence laughed.

'Ooh, Miss Giggle today, are we?' said Dougal.

'I'm sure I don't know what you mean,' said Florence. 'And now . . . what's happening in the garden?'

'You may well ask,' said Dougal, darkly.

'Yes, you may well ask,' said Ermintrude, sadly.

'It's pathetic,' said Dougal, 'pathetic.'

'What's wrong?' said Florence.

'Toothache,' said Dougal.

'You poor thing,' said Florence, to Ermintrude.

'It's dreadful,' said Ermintrude, '*dreadful*.'

'Too many sweeties,' said Dougal.

'I never touch them,' said Ermintrude.

'We must *do* something,' said Florence.

'What had you in mind?' said Dougal.

At that moment, Brian arrived and it just so happened he had some lettuce juice with him. Florence gave some to Ermintrude as Brian said it would give immediate relief.

'Er . . . any immediate relief?' said Brian.

'No,' said Ermintrude.

Dougal was rather scathing about the lettuce juice . . .

'Cures warts,' said Brian.

'But we're not curing warts, are we,' said Dougal. 'We're curing toothache . . . great clump!'

'Well what?' said Florence.

'Let me think,' said Dougal.

'Pull it out with string,' said Brian. 'An old country remedy.'

'String?' said Dougal.

'Stir-*ring*,' said Brian.

The next problem was to find string . . .

Brian approaches a sleeping Dylan, circles him, and attempts to pluck a string from his guitar.

'Like . . . what?' said Dylan. *He sighs and snores.*

'That's no good,' said Dougal.

'I did my best,' said Brian. 'Ten out of ten for effort, anyway.'

Florence had an idea.

She sees Penelope's web and unravels a small part of it . . .

'I'll just borrow some web . . . I hope Penelope won't

mind,' said Florence.

'All the same if she does now,' said Dougal.

'Be quiet, Dougal, and tie it on,' said Florence.

So Dougal did.

'Right, prepare to *heave*,' he said.

'*Heave?*' said Ermintrude, faintly.

'Just relax,' said Dougal. 'Now *heave! . . . Heave!*'

Ermintrude moos, rather distressed.

'Any good?' said Florence.

'No,' said Dougal.

'Total failure,' said Brian and Ermintrude.

'I seem to remember my Auntie Maisie tying the string to a door handle,' said Dougal. 'Let's give it a whirl.'

And he ties one end of the string to his door. He leaves, Ermintrude walks away, and the door crashes to the ground.

'It's a funny thing,' said Ermintrude, 'but it doesn't ache any more.'

The Mysterious Beast

Mr Rusty told Florence he was thinking of going with her to the garden.

'Everyone ready?' said Zebedee, and when Florence said she was, they went.

'I don't want to worry you,' said Dougal, 'but if I were you I'd leave straight away.'

'Why?' asked Florence and Mr Rusty, surprised.

'*Because*,' said Dougal.

But Florence and Mr Rusty didn't think that was much of an answer.

'Ah well,' said Dougal, 'don't say I didn't warn you.'

Brian arrived looking rather agitated.

'Run for your lives,' he said.

'What are you talking about, mollusc?' said Dougal. 'Pathetic creature.'

'There's a monster in the garden,' said Brian. 'I mean – another one, besides you.'

'A monster?' said Mr Rusty.

'A fearsome monster,' said Brian.

Ermintrude appeared – also in some agitation. 'A monster,' she said.

'I knew this was going to be a bad day,' said Dougal.

'We must flee,' said Ermintrude.

'It's got horns,' said Brian.

'And a tail,' said Ermintrude.

'And it snorts and hisses,' they said.

In fact, they made it sound so fearsome the others went quite pale.

'Produce your monster,' said Dougal.

But Brian and Ermintrude said they'd rather not see it again, it was so frightening.

'We'll go and find it,' said Florence.

'Are you mad?' said Dougal.

Florence and Mr Rusty go off in search of the mysterious beast.

'Listen!!' shrieked Brian.

'That's the best monster I've ever seen,' said Mr Rusty.

'They've gone near it,' said Dougal, faintly.

'Very brave,' said Ermintrude.

'Foolhardy,' said Brian.

Florence and Mr Rusty discussed the monster.

'What do you think?' said Florence.

'Centipede?' said Mr Rusty. 'Er . . . big centipede.'

'It's getting ready to pounce,' said Dougal, 'I can tell.'

'I can't look,' said Brian. 'It's too fearsome for little me.'

But when the monster didn't move, their curiosity got the better of them and they went to have a closer look.

'Don't you think there's something familiar about it, dear boy?' said Ermintrude.

'I hope it doesn't get familiar with *me*,' said Dougal, 'because I'm feeling a bit frail today and if that thing makes a move towards me, I may scream and faint.'

The creature made a move . . .

. . . and the group scattered.

'Were you all terrified?' said the train, and they all

said they certainly were.

'Except me,' said Dougal. 'I knew it was a train. It had to be a train – what else could it have been but a train? It was quite obviously a train – quite obvious. A train . . . It couldn't have been more like a train. I mean . . . it was . . . a train . . . a train.'

Ermintrude's Folly

'Hello,' said Mr Rusty.

'Hello,' said Florence.

'Just giving the old barrel a turn,' said Mr Rusty.

'I heard it,' said Florence.

Zebedee arrived.

'Shall we go?' said Florence.

'Why not?' said Zebedee.

'Yes, why not?' said Florence.

In the garden, she looked for Dougal . . . who was looking for *her*. Somewhat agitatedly . . .

'There you are! Ooh, I'm very glad to see you. I can't tell you how glad I am to see you,' said Dougal.

'Why?' said Florence.

'Oh, I wish you hadn't asked me that!' said Dougal, 'because I don't know how to break it to you. I know you're very fond of her . . .'

'Who?' said Florence.

'Who? Oh, I don't think I should tell you, you know . . . Oh dear, oh dear, oh dear . . . oh dear . . . oh dear.'

'*Who*, Dougal?' said Florence.

'Ermintrude. I'm afraid she's been affected by all those poppies she's been eating,' said Dougal.

'Poppies?' said Florence.

'Well, it's either that or the pansies – I don't know which is worse,' said Dougal. 'But whatever it is the poor old thing's in a very bad way. I think her moon-jumping days are over, anyway. If she ever did it – which I doubt. It's always seemed a very unlikely story to me.'

'Dougal,' said Florence, 'would you kindly tell me what this is all about.'

'All right,' said Dougal. 'That cow is flying a kite.'

'A kite?' said Florence.

'A kite!' said Dougal. 'C-I-T-E. Kite. She is flying a kite.'

'How lovely,' said Florence.

'Lovely?' said Dougal. 'It's unnatural. Cows don't fly kites. Cows eat grass and do a lot of mooing and lying about in fields and things of that nature.'

'Well, perhaps she felt like a change,' said Florence.

'That's hardly a reason to fly a kite,' said Dougal.

And they set off to meet the kite-flyer.

'I've brought you a few flowers to nibble,' said Dougal.

'Bless you, dear boy,' said Ermintrude.

'What are you doing?' said Dougal.

'I'm flying my kite,' said Ermintrude. 'Very relaxing . . . Would you like to have a try?'

'Er . . . that's very kind of you,' said Dougal.

'Hold on tight,' said Ermintrude – with reason.

'What – what!' said Dougal.

Dougal rises into the air at an alarming rate . . .

'Help, help!' said Dougal.

'It's a very good kite,' said Ermintrude, laughing. 'I do hope he doesn't lose it.'

'I hope we don't lose Dougal,' said Florence.

'Oh, don't worry, dear thing,' said Ermintrude. 'He'll come down to earth eventually.'

'Help! Help!' said Dougal.

Dougal, eventually, hits the ground with a CRASH!

Florence rushed to the scene. 'All right, Dougal?' she said.

'You cannot imagine,' said Dougal, 'how infuriating a question like that can be when you've just been up in a kite and crashed.'

At the Door Department

Zebedee told Florence that Dougal seemed to be having a bit of trouble in the garden. This didn't surprise Florence greatly, but she said she would go and see.

'I wonder what it is this time?' she mused, and when Dougal arrived she asked him.

'Well, it's this letter,' said Dougal. 'It's got me all upset . . .'

So Florence read it. 'Dear Sir, Your rent is overdue. Pay up or else. Your obedient servant . . . Hm!' said Florence.

'Obedient servant!' said Dougal. 'I like that.'

'The point *is*,' said Florence, 'what are we going to do? It's a very desperate situation.'

'It most certainly *is*,' said Dougal.

'Have you got any money?' said Florence.

'Money? I despise it!' said Dougal.

'Pity,' said Florence.

Brian arrived and Florence told him about Dougal's problem.

'I'll be arrested,' said Dougal. 'How humiliating.'

'Then don't let them in?' said Brian.

'You know,' said Dougal, 'that snail's right. I shall get a gate.'

By the oddest of coincidences, there were some gates in the garden, all of them guaranteed to keep out unwanted visitors . . .

Dougal was delighted. 'The very thing,' he said.

'Get your gates here,' said the gate. 'Latest things in gates and doors. All guaranteed against burglars and moths.'

Dylan appeared to be in charge . . .

Dylan rises and yawns.

'Ignore him,' said Dougal.

They looked round . . .

'I am a little gate,' said the little gate. 'But jolly useful.'

'Come on,' said Dougal.

'I am a big gate,' said the big gate. 'I keep out anything.'

'Not quite true, dear thing,' said Ermintrude, walking through the gate.

'That's no good,' said Dougal.

'Gates *are* no good,' said Ermintrude. 'If one is determined enough. Ha! Ha! Like me.'

Ermintrude falls and cries out.

'That's perfect,' said Dougal, laughing. 'That 's exactly right. I'll get one of those.'

'I appear to have fallen down a hole,' said Ermintrude, echoing.

'She's right, you know,' said Dougal, and Florence put the lid on it.

'I say, that's a bit heartless, isn't it?' said Dougal.

'She seemed quite comfy,' said Florence.

They met something else . . . 'Who are you?' said Dougal.

'I am a portable wall,' said the wall. 'With me you can always feel safe. Guaranteed against floods and field mice.'

'Useful if we have some rain,' said Dougal.

'Or field mice,' said Florence.

'But it's not getting me far with my problem,' said Dougal.

So they went to see some more gates and doors . . . and they found one which seemed to Dougal to be just right.

'This seems all right,' he said. 'Functional and pretty . . . like me. Oh, yes . . . lovely . . . that'll keep them out,' said Dougal, laughing.

Dougal gets caught on the gate.

'Ooh! Not me, you dolt! . . . I think it might be safer to pay the rent,' said Dougal.

Ermintrude's Hat
– Part 1

In the garden a problem had arisen and it was nothing to do with flowers. . .

Florence met Dougal.

'We've got a problem,' he said. 'A *big* problem.'

'Can I help?' said Florence.

'Well, if you can't, nobody can,' said Dougal. 'It's a very *feminine* problem. Are you good at choosing hats?'

'Very good,' said Florence.

'For cows?' said Dougal.

'I need a new hat,' said Ermintrude.

'I'll say,' said Dougal.

'And I want something very chic,' said Ermintrude.

'How about a trilby?' said Dougal.

'Dougal!' said Florence.

'Sorry,' said Dougal.

'Can you help?' said Ermintrude.

And Dougal and Florence said they would do their best to find Ermintrude a new hat.

They met Brian and explained the problem.

'We need to find some hats,' they said.

'I'll help,' said Brian.

'That'll be the day,' said Dougal.

Fortunately, Brian's help wasn't needed, for just then a large group of hats appeared before them . . .

'Do you see what I see?' said Dougal.

'Get your hats here,' said the hat. 'Hats for h'all occasions. If you don't see what you want, just ask. Satisfaction guaranteed, estimates free . . .'

'Bit noisy wearing that one,' said Dougal.

'I am a *gay* hat,' said another hat.

'I wouldn't dispute that,' said Brian.

'But is it a *cow* hat?' said Dougal.

Florence asked the hat if it had anything suitable for a cow and the hat got a bit flustered.

'A cow?' It shuddered.

'A *spotted* cow,' said Dougal.

'Spotted?' said the hat.

'*Spotted!*' they said.

'And difficult to please,' said Dougal.

'How about me?' said the fur hat. 'I'm very warm, all purpose . . . and incredibly expensive . . .'

'Do you think that's *her*?' said Dougal.

'No, it's *fur*,' said Brian.

'Try not to provoke me,' said Dougal.

'How about me?' said a cap. 'I will give yer years of faithful service and I can be used for golf, cricket, fishing, swatting flies and carrying chips.'

'The Mad Hatter was *nothing* on this,' said Dougal, '*nothing.*'

'How about me?' said another hat. 'I am small and elegent for a small and elegant head . . .'

'That's me?' said Brian, and Florence laughed.

'This,' said Dougal, 'is getting us nowhere.'

'What do you suggest?' said Florence.

'I suggest we forget the whole business,' said Dougal. 'Hats for cows, really!'

'Well, she did *ask*, Dougal,' said Florence.

'Well I suggest we put it off until tomorrow,' said Dougal. 'All these hats are giving me a headache.'

'Anyone in there?' said Brian.

Ermintrude's Hat – Part 2

Florence told Mr Rusty what a difficult time they'd had trying to find a new hat for Ermintrude and Mr Rusty said that it wasn't a task to be undertaken lightly.

'No, indeed,' said Florence.

Zebedee arrived. 'Any luck with the new hat?' he asked.

'No,' said Florence.

'Cows aren't easy to please,' said Mr Rusty.

'I shall have to go and try again,' said Florence, going.

'I don't wish to seem dog in the manger about this,' said Dougal, 'but couldn't that cow *knit* herself a new hat? I could lend her my needles . . .'

'No,' said Florence, 'we *must* find her one.'

'But what does she want a hat for anyway?' said Dougal. 'It doesn't do anything for her.'

But Florence said it was no use arguing – she had promised and she was going to find one.

Ermintrude should have her new hat.

'We're going to regret this,' grumped Dougal.

'Stop mumbling, Dougal,' said Florence.

'Here we go then,' said Dougal. 'Sort this little lot out.'

'I am very smart,' said a French boater. 'Very suitable for man, or woman or cow . . . Every little breeze . . . seems to whisper Louise,' sang the hat.

'I knew this would be difficult,' said Dougal, sighing.

'Hello, darlings,' said a rather sultry, wide hat. 'Looking for something just a little bit different? Just a little bit outré . . . hmm?'

'That's about as suitable for a cow as a kilt,' said Dougal. 'If she wears that she'll be drummed out of the herd.'

Another hat appeared . . .

'I am suitable for a wedding,' it said. 'Is the cow to be married?'

'We don't think so,' said Florence.

'Then I wish you wouldn't waste my time,' said the hat, tartly.

'Hoity-toity!' said Dougal.

Yet another hat appeared . . .

'It *is* difficult, isn't it?' said Florence.

'Well, you wouldn't listen, would you?' said Dougal.

Another hat tried . . .

'Will the wearer be going to Ascot? Or the Royal Garden Party . . . or *Cowes*,' said the hat, laughing.

'No, it's more for everyday wear,' said Florence.

'Every *day*?!' said the hat.

'Yes,' said Florence.

'Then excuse *me*,' said the hat.

'Oh, come on,' said Dougal. 'It's hopeless.'

'One more try,' said Florence.

'I want to be *alone*,' said their last hope.

'You're likely to be,' said Dougal, 'looking like *that*.'

But Florence thought it was just the thing and she gave it to Ermintrude.

It fitted perfectly, which wasn't surprising, for it was Ermintrude's old hat which she had taken to a jumble sale in aid of destitute dogs.

'Destitute dogs?' said Dougal. 'Why wasn't I invited. I'm about as destitute as you can get.'

'I think it's about time for bed,' said Florence.

'It's been an exhausting couple of days,' said Dougal.

'I want to be alone,' said Ermintrude.

La Tombola

Florence and Mr Rusty were waiting for Zebedee.

'He's late,' said Mr Rusty.

'As usual,' said Florence.

'Am I late?' said Zebedee, sweetly.

'Yes,' said Florence. 'Kindly explain.'

So Zebedee explained that he'd been having a look round and there seemed to be something happening in the garden she might be interested in . . .

'But of course if you're angry with me for being late, you probably don't want to go,' he said.

'Oh, you!' said Florence.

'She's late,' said Dougal. 'Children nowadays – really!'

'Am I late?' said Florence.

'Not at all, dear thing,' said Ermintrude, much to Dougal's disgust. 'There's too much "rush, rush, rush" these days. Everyone rushes about like a bull at a gate . . . er, what am I saying! But be that as it may, *I* shall take my time and browse along . . . and, you never know, the odd flower may find itself chomped as I go but at least I won't *rush* . . .' said Ermintrude, laughing. 'I shall strike a blow for *leisure*.'

Brian was running a raffle. 'It's in aid of shipwrecked snails,' he said, 'and I want you all to buy a ticket. One carrot each.'

'You're joking,' said Dougal.

Mr MacHenry bought one.

'Very wise,' said Brian, 'and I hope you will be a lucky winner of a wonderful prize.'

Dylan bought one as well.

'When's the draw?' they said.

'When I've sold all the tickets,' said Brian.

'That'll be the day,' said Dougal.

But Florence bought one.

'I wouldn't trust that snail with a train ticket,' said Dougal.

'Isn't it exciting?' said Florence.

'Huh!' said Dougal.

'I wonder if I'll win,' said Florence, hopefully.

'All right then, any more for any more?' said Brian.

'Oh, get on with it,' said Dougal. 'Great oaf!'

'Want a ticket then?' said Brian.

'No, I do not,' said Dougal.

'Oh, go on,' said Brian, 'be a sport.'

'You might win something, Dougal,' said Florence.

And the others urged Dougal to get a ticket . . . so finally he did.

'Congratulations!' said Brian.

'All right then,' said Dougal, 'what happens now?'

'Do we choose our prize?' said Florence.

'Not *quite*,' said Brian. 'Not *quite*.'

'I knew there'd be a catch in it,' said Dougal.

Florence read her ticket carefully.

'What's it say?' said Dougal.

'It says "This ticket must be given up in return for laundry",' said Florence.

'So does mine!' said Mr MacHenry.

'I knew it!' said Dougal. 'The rogue!'

'But it also says there's a special prize for the lucky number,' said Florence.

'Lucky number of *what*?' said Dougal.

'Ah,' said Brian.

'Oh, look!' said Florence, spotting a parcel. 'That must be the prize.'

Dougal inspected.

'I wonder what's in there? A year's supply of lettuce?' said Dougal, laughing.

'Yoo! Hoo!' said Ermintrude, jumping out of the parcel. 'You know, I've always wanted to do that.'

'Well, that's the prize,' said Brian. 'Ticket number *four*.'

'Ticket number *four*?' gasped Dougal.

'And the lucky winner gets a kiss,' said Ermintrude.

Dougal jumps into the parcel, and seals himself in.

'Where are you, dear thing?' said Ermintrude.

'I've gone abroad,' said Dougal with an echo.

Painting the Roundabout

Zebedee was waiting for Florence in the wrong place.

Funny, he thought, it's not like her to be late . . .

Florence wasn't late – she was talking to Mr Rusty and waiting for Zebedee.

'I was waiting in the wrong place,' said Zebedee.

'That's all right,' said Florence.

'Did you miss me?' said Zebedee.

'No,' said Florence.

'Oh, you're awful,' said Zebedee.

'We want to paint the Roundabout,' said Florence, and Zebedee thought this was a good idea.

'Can you help?' said Florence.

'I don't see why not,' said Zebedee. 'What sort of help would you require . . . ?'

'Well, we need brushes and paint,' said Mr Rusty. 'Quite a lot of paint and . . . brushes.'

'Well, that shouldn't be too difficult,' said Zebedee.

'And painters,' said Florence.

'In that case,' said Zebedee, 'we'd better take the Roundabout to the garden with us.'

'Oh, can you do that?' said Florence.

'I don't wish to boast,' said Zebedee, 'but I can do anything, provided it's not too difficult . . . and it is only a *little* roundabout.'

And he laughed and they left, taking the Roundabout with them.

Dougal was amazed.

'Er . . . do you know you've got a roundabout with you?' he said.

'Yes, we do,' said Florence.

'We're going to paint it,' said Mr Rusty. 'And we need everyone's help.'

'Everyone,' said Florence.

'You probably need a bit of paint as well,' said Dougal, laughing.

'True,' said Florence.

Luckily, Ermintrude had some paint . . .

'I mixed it specially, dear things,' she said.

Mr Rusty hoped it was a nice bright colour and Dougal had a look.

'What sort of paint *is* this?' he asked.

'It's paint paint,' said Ermintrude. 'Made of paint . . .'

'What do you think?' said Dougal.

'Don't know,' said Florence.

But Mr Rusty said he was sure the paint was all right and they should get started.

So they did.

'Looks brighter,' said Mr Rusty.

'Much brighter,' said Florence.

'I've got a funny feeling,' said Dougal, 'that we're not getting anywhere.'

'How's it going?' said Ermintrude. 'It looks *lovely*.'

'All sparkling and beautiful,' said Ermintrude.

'I have a question,' said Dougal.

'Yes, dear heart?' said Ermintrude.

'What's in this paint?' said Dougal.

'Yes, what's it made of?' said Florence.

'Water, of course,' said Ermintrude.

'Just water?' said Mr Rusty. He looked at the Round-about. 'Ah well, it needed a wash, anyway, and you can't expect a cow to mix paint, can you?'

Once Upon a Time

Dougal met Brian.

'Greetings, fat and furry fiend,' said Brian.

'The word is "friend",' said Dougal.

'Oh, I don't know,' said Brian.

'Watch your step, snail,' said Dougal.

'I can't . . . I've got no feet,' said Brian.

'Not a leg to stand on, eh?' giggled Dougal.

'Don't mock,' said Brian.

And they went on like this for some time, much to the amusement of Ermintrude, who was hiding . . .

'Moo!' said Ermintrude.

'What on earth was that?' said Dougal.

'I don't want to know,' said Brian.

They met Florence and told her about the terrible noise they had heard in the garden.

'What sort of noise?' she said.

'Ghastly,' said Dougal.

'Like the Hound of the Boskyvilles,' said Brian.

'I must investigate,' said Florence.

Florence bravely strides off to investigate, then stops.

'Er . . . after you,' said Florence.

'After us?' said Dougal. 'You must be joking.'

'Yes, we've heard it,' squeaked Brian.

So Florence rethought the situation. 'You're very-

cowardly,' she said. 'After all, I'm a lady.'

'I don't see what that's got to do with it,' said Dougal.

'Don't you?' said Brian.

'No, I do not!' said Dougal.

'MOO!!!' said Ermintrude.

'There it is again!' screeched Dougal.

'Don't you know who that is?' said Florence.

'No, we don't,' said Brian.

'And we don't want to,' said Dougal.

'I shall write to the Noise Abatement Society,' said Brian.

Ermintrude, very pleased with the chaos she had created, tried it out on Dylan.

'MOO!!' she said.

'Hi, mam!' said Dylan.

'Come with me!' said Ermintrude.

So Dylan went.

'Watch,' whispered Ermintrude, 'MOO!!'

'I can't stand it! I can't stand it!' said Dougal.

'Steady, Dougal,' said Florence.

'Don't crack up,' said Brian.

Dylan wasn't too sure about Ermintrude's joke. 'Mam,' he said. 'I'm not sure that dog can stand the strain. He's . . . like . . . neurotic and you may crack him up.'

Ermintrude was very contrite. 'You may be right,' she said. 'I won't do it again . . . I promise.'

'Great,' said Dylan and Ermintrude left, sighing.

Dylan felt a bit sorry for her and thought he'd pick her a few flowers as a present.

'Fun while it lasted,' said Ermintrude, and then saw something quite strange. A moving tree. 'Moo, moo.'

But it was only Dylan with his present – a small tree and some flowers.

'Moo,' said Ermintrude.

And she eats the flowers, while Dylan has a restorative sleep.

Dylan woke up, found that part of his present had gone, forgot it and went to sleep again.

Ermintrude was at it again . . .

'MOO!!' said Ermintrude.

'It's at it again,' said Brian.

'I'm a husk,' said Dougal. 'No one will know what I suffer.'

'Moo!' said Ermintrude.

'You!' said Brian.

'Yes,' said Ermintrude. 'Well, I've got to have fun sometimes . . .'

Golf and an Omelette

Florence was in the garden waiting for Zebedee, when Brian came along.

'I have come,' he said, 'to take you to where the action is. Merriment and mirth is in store for you.'

'Dougal?' said Florence.

'How did you guess?' said Brian, laughing. 'Old shaggy breeks is at it again and we are all invited.'

They leave to take up their invitations for merriment and mirth, and soon meet their host.

'What is it?' said Florence.

'Golf!' said Dougal. 'The royal and ancient game at which I excel. Now, if you all pay strict attention I will explain the rules and show you some of the finer points . . . all right?'

'Is it true you taught Tony Jacklin?' said Brian.

'I shall ignore that,' said Dougal. 'Now, where was I? Er . . . er . . .'

'The finer points, man,' said Dylan.

'Oh, yes,' said Dougal, 'the finer points.'

Dylan dropped off while Dougal went on . . . and on.

'We didn't quite follow,' they said.

'Really,' said Dougal.

'Perhaps a demonstration,' said Florence.

'All in good time,' said Dougal. 'Golf cannot be

hurried – it's not like marbles . . .'

'Now there's a game for experts, man,' said Dylan. 'Marbles . . . great game.'

'How did marbles get into this?' said Dougal. 'Who on earth's talking about marbles?'

'*You* are,' they said.

Dougal got quite confused. 'Oooh . . . Now I'm confused,' he said.

'Compose yourself, dear thing,' said Ermintrude.

'What?' said Dougal.

'Composure,' said Ermintrude.

'I *am* composured,' said Dougal.

'I think we should get on,' said Florence.

'Oh, all right,' said Dougal. 'Impatient lot . . .'

'Marbles is a great game,' said Dylan.

'I'll do that rabbit an injury,' said Dougal.

'Oh, get teed up,' said Brian, and they all agreed that it was about time Dougal stopped talking and started playing, otherwise, as Florence said, they'd be playing golf in the dark . . .

'Oh, all right,' said Dougal.

'Oh good,' said Florence.

Dougal's first shot went into the rough . . .

'Yes, well, that's what *not* to do,' said Dougal with a cough. 'Now watch carefully . . .'

But his second ball missed the hole as well. How humiliating, he thought.

Dylan had a go . . .

. . . *and the ball flies unerringly into the hole.*

'Bravo!' said Florence.

Dylan had another go . . .

'Bravo!' they said.

Dougal tried hard . . . and this time he was successful, to everyone's surprise.

'I did it! I did it!' said Dougal.

Dougal looks in the hole . . .

'Where is it?' said Dougal.

'Where are the others?' said Florence.

Everyone looked everywhere, but not, oddly enough, in the right place, which was Mr MacHenry's basket.

'Hello all,' he said.

'How did you get those?' said Dougal, sternly.

'I was in my garden and they appeared,' said Mr MacHenry. 'Eggs, aren't they? I shall cook them later. . .'

'Yes! Boil them!' said Brian, giggling.

'Well, that's that,' said Florence. 'Good-night.'

I don't think I quite understood that game, thought Ermintrude.

The Relay Race

Florence told Mr Rusty that she felt energetic and Mr Rusty said he thought that was a very good way to feel – in moderation, of course.

'But it's a long time since I felt energetic,' he said. 'Very long time.'

'Oh?' said Florence.

'But I was very good at the hop, skip and jump in my youth,' said Mr Rusty. 'Very good indeed.'

'I'd like to have seen that,' said Florence.

'It was a sight, I can tell you,' said Mr Rusty. 'A rare sight. People came for miles to see me do the hop, skip and jump . . . A rare sight. A rare old sight . . .'

'Don't you do it any more?' said Florence.

'Not a lot,' said Mr Rusty.

Zebedee arrived. 'Everyone feeling energetic?' he said, 'because there are great things going on in the garden.'

'Right, everyone here?' said Dougal. 'Then I'll begin. Today, as you know, is the day of the great race.'

'I didn't know,' said Florence.

'You're not the only one, dear heart,' said Ermintrude.

'Well, I know,' said Brian, 'and I am the very popular captain of my team which consists of one snail, one rabbit and one cow. It is a race against the clock – one lap of the track and no using bicycles. All right? Everyone understand?'

Dougal set the clock . . .

'We each have to carry something,' said Brian.

'Perhaps someone would care to carry *me*,' said Ermintrude, 'I'm quite light . . .'

'Now stop messing about,' said Dougal.

'Sorry, dear thing,' said Ermintrude.

'Who's going to start?' said Brian.

'I will,' said Florence.

'Go then,' said Brian.

And Florence went.

'Stop!' said Dougal.

'Something wrong?' said Florence.

'You didn't say ready-steady,' said Dougal.

'Oh, Mr Perfection!' said Brian, heavily. 'Ready! Steady! Go!'

And Florence went again.

Mr Rusty, who had to go next, waited nervously for Florence to come back, checked it was really his turn, and set off, showing some of his old hop, skip and jump vigour.

'Bravo!' said Ermintrude. 'Who would have thought he had it in him?'

Dylan wondered if he'd stay awake long enough to take part.

'Play up!' said Ermintrude.

And Dylan played up. 'I'm not sure I can finish the course,' said Dylan, yawning. 'I'm . . . like . . . exhausted.'

But Zebedee was a flying umpire . . . and Dylan found he had to go.

'Whose turn?' said Brian.

'It's *you*, snail, dear!' said Ermintrude.

And Brian showed them what he was made of . . . with a little help from Zebedee, like pointing him in the right direction.

Dougal waited . . . and then set off.

He got a little side-tracked by a pile of sugar.

'Ooh! The temptations they put in your way these days . . . oooh! What shall I do?' said Dougal.

'Remember the team!' said Zebedee.

'Oh . . . oh? The team?' said Dougal.

'What's keeping him, I wonder,' said Ermintrude, and when Dougal came back, off she went.

'Oh, I do feel a fool,' she said.

Zebedee said they'd wait for Ermintrude to get back and then decide the winner. Ermintrude did finally get back and Zebedee declared her the winner.

'I owe my victory to clean living and vegetarianism,' said Ermintrude, with a cough.

Cup and Ball

Florence met Dylan . . .

'Hi, mam!' he said. 'See what I have here. It's a game of skill.'

Florence examined it. There was a ball and a spike and the idea was to get the ball on the spike.

'I did it!' she said.

'Well done,' said Dylan.

'Can you do it?' said Florence.

But Dylan told her he'd been trying to do it for so long he was exhausted and all he needed was a long sleep – if he could find somewhere comfortable to rest his head. Somewhere shady and secluded – where he was not likely to be disturbed.

And he immediately falls asleep and starts to snore.

He found the ideal place.

Meanwhile, Florence got quite skilled at Dylan's game of skill.

'Tiptoe, thru' the tulips . . .' said Ermintrude.

'Ermintrude,' said Florence.

'Yes, dear heart?' said Ermintrude.

'Look!' said Florence.

'Good heavens!' said Ermintrude.

'It's quite a game,' said Florence.

'Yes,' said Ermintrude.

'And I'm very skilled at it,' said Florence.

'Showing off rather a lot,' said Brian. 'What you got?'

'It's a game of skill,' said Florence, 'at which I am very skilled.'

'Clever old you,' said Brian.

'Want a go?' said Florence.

'No thanks,' said Brian.

'Why not, snaily dear?' said Ermintrude.

'Bit tricky without hands,' said Brian.

And Florence was forced to agree – it would be tricky without hands.

'What games do you play, dear thing?' said Ermintrude.

'I don't really,' said Brian.

'Nothing?' said Ermintrude.

'Well, a bit of skiing now and again,' said Brian.

'Funny little fellow,' said Ermintrude, laughing. 'But I do like him.'

'Oh, and hopscotch,' said Brian.

Dougal had a go.

'Well done, Dougal,' said Florence.

'Not difficult,' said Dougal.

'I know,' said Florence.

Zebedee wanted to know what was going on . . . so Florence told him.

'Can I try?' he asked.

So Florence said of course he could.

Ermintrude and Brian felt a bit left out of it . . .

'Well, I'm glad everyone's enjoying themselves,' said Ermintrude. 'Come along, small creature.'

'Where we going, then?' said Brian. 'Up the pictures? Watch the Magic Roundabout on the telly? I like that.'

'No, we're going to play a game,' said Ermintrude.

'Ooh! A game!' said Brian. 'Alley oop!'
Brian jumps in the air and lands heavily.

'Ow!' said Brian.

Sparrow-Weed

Zebedee was in the garden wondering what had happened to everyone.

What's happened to everyone? he thought.

And he asked Mr Rusty.

'What's happened to everyone?' he said.

'I'm here,' said Mr Rusty.

'But you're not everyone,' said Zebedee. 'Are you?'

'No,' said Mr Rusty.

So Zebedee decided to go and see where everyone was (and what they were doing).

Florence was talking to a bird, and the bird told her that his name was Stanley and he was feeling rather hungry.

'There's a particular seed in a particular flower that I like to eat and I can't find it anywhere,' he said.

'It's called a sparrow-weed and I do like it,' he said.

'Sparrow-weed?' said Florence.

'Sparrow-weed?' said Zebedee.

'I'll help you find some if you like,' said Florence. 'I'm sure there's some in the garden.'

And Stanley said he'd be very grateful. 'Shall we walk or fly?' he said.

'We'll have to walk, I think,' said Florence, and she borrowed Mr Rusty's hat, put the bird inside it . . . and went to look for some sparrow-weed.

What's this? thought Dougal, watching Florence's

search from behind a tree.

'What's this?' he said. 'What are you doing with Mr Rusty's hat? Explain!'

So Florence told Dougal about Stanley and how he was hungry.

'Yes,' said Dougal. 'Does look a bit peaky. Distinctly peaky.'

And Florence asked Dougal to help to look for some sparrow-weed.

'All right,' said Dougal.

'Thank you,' said Stanley.

So Dougal asked everyone if they knew where to find some sparrow-weed.

'Never touch the stuff,' said the other birds.

'Hello, handsome,' said the cow.

'Can I help?' said Brian, joining the group of searchers.

'We're looking for some sparrow-weed,' said Florence.

'Never touch the stuff,' said Brian.

'But can you find us some?' said Florence, getting a little impatient.

'Plenty about,' said the birds.

'Where?' said Florence.

'Plenty about,' said Ermintrude.

'Where?' said Dougal.

'Where?' said Florence.

'Where?' said Dougal.

'Where?' said Florence.

'I'll show you,' said Ermintrude.

But Zebedee said there wasn't time.

'Nothing's easy,' said Florence, sighing.